My First Sleepover

By Lauren Cecil
Illustrated by Terry Workman

Grosset & Dunlap
An Imprint of Penguin Group (USA) Inc.

GROSSET & DUNLAP
Published by the Penguin Group
Penguin Group (USA) Inc., 375 Hudson Street,
New York, New York 10014, USA
Penguin Group (Canada), 90 Eglinton Avenue East, Suite 700,
Toronto, Ontario M4P 2Y3, Canada
(a division of Pearson Penguin Canada Inc.)
Penguin Books Ltd., 80 Strand, London WC2R 0RL, England
Penguin Group Ireland, 25 St. Stephen's Green, Dublin 2, Ireland
(a division of Penguin Books Ltd.)
Penguin Group (Australia), 250 Camberwell Road, Camberwell, Victoria 3124, Australia
(a division of Pearson Australia Group Pty. Ltd.)
Penguin Books India Pvt. Ltd., 11 Community Centre,
Panchsheel Park, New Delhi—110 017, India
Penguin Group (NZ), 67 Apollo Drive, Rosedale, Auckland 0632, New Zealand
(a division of Pearson New Zealand Ltd.)
Penguin Books (South Africa) (Pty.) Ltd., 24 Sturdee Avenue,
Rosebank, Johannesburg 2196, South Africa

Penguin Books Ltd., Registered Offices:
80 Strand, London WC2R 0RL, England

Strawberry Shortcake™ and related trademarks © 2010, 2012 Those Characters From Cleveland, Inc. Used under license by
Penguin Young Readers Group. All rights reserved. This edition published in 2012 as part of the *Strawberry Shortcake: A Berry Best Collection*
gift set by Grosset & Dunlap, a division of Penguin Young Readers Group, 345 Hudson Street, New York, New York 10014.
GROSSET & DUNLAP is a trademark of Penguin Group (USA) Inc. Manufactured in China.

Gift Set ISBN 978-0-448-46290-5   10 9 8 7 6 5 4 3 2 1

One afternoon, Strawberry Shortcake was shopping
at Raspberry Torte's store.

As Strawberry was looking through the pajamas, she got a great idea.
"We should have a sleepover party!" Strawberry said excitedly.

"A sleepover?" asked Raspberry. She didn't sound as excited as Strawberry.
"Yes! It'll be berry fun," said Strawberry. "We can invite all our friends."

The next day, all the girls went to Strawberry's café to plan the sleepover party.

"We can have the party at my bookstore," said Blueberry Muffin.

"I'll bring music," said Plum Pudding.

"I can bring a movie," said Orange Blossom.
"I can bring stuff for makeovers," said Lemon Meringue.
"And I can bring snacks!" added Strawberry.

"Raspberry, what do you want to bring?" Strawberry asked.

"I'm really busy at my store," said Raspberry. "I don't think I have time to help."

"That's okay," said Strawberry. "All you need to bring is yourself!"

The day before the party, Strawberry's phone rang.
"I'm not feeling well," Raspberry said. "I don't think
I can come to the sleepover."

Strawberry was worried. She and all her friends went to see Raspberry. "Are you all right?" Strawberry asked.

"Every time we talk about the sleepover, my stomach feels all funny and my head gets dizzy," admitted Raspberry.

10

"Hmmm," said Blueberry. "Have you ever been to a sleepover?"
"Never," answered Raspberry shyly.
"Maybe you feel sick because you're nervous about doing something new," Orange said.

"Maybe you're right," said Raspberry. "I don't know if I will like sleepovers. What if I get homesick?"

"Bring your favorite stuffed animal with you," said Orange. "It will remind you of home."

"What if I wake up in the middle of the night?" Raspberry asked.
"Think of your favorite story until you fall back asleep," Plum said.

"And if those things don't work, you can go home whenever you want," Strawberry said.

"Okay," Raspberry agreed. "I'll give sleepovers a try."

On the day of the party, Raspberry packed up her things and went to Blueberry's bookstore. She was still a little nervous.

"Hi, Raspberry!" Blueberry said. "I'm so glad you're here. We're going to have lots of fun!"

First, the girls danced to their favorite songs.
Raspberry loved bopping to the beat!

Then the girls snacked on Strawberry's triple-berry muffins.
Yum, thought Raspberry. *Strawberry's muffins are berry-licious!*

After that, the girls gave one another makeovers.

Raspberry giggled when she saw her new look!

At the end of the night, the girls curled up and watched a movie.

When the movie was over, Strawberry asked, "Raspberry, are you having fun?" But Raspberry didn't answer. She was already asleep!

In the morning, the girls went to Strawberry's café for breakfast. As they ate, Strawberry asked Raspberry, "What did you think of your first sleepover?"

"It was great," Raspberry answered. "But there was one problem . . ."
"Oh no!" Strawberry gasped. "What went wrong?"

"It was over too soon!" said Raspberry. "I had so much fun! I can't wait until we do it again!"